This book belongs to

......................................

Quarto is the authority on a wide range of topics.

Quarto educates, entertains and enriches the lives of our readers—enthusiasts and lovers of hands-on living.

www.quartoknows.com

© 2018 Quarto Publishing plc

First published in 2018 by QED Publishing, an imprint of The Quarto Group. The Old Brewery, 6 Blundell Street, London N7 9BH, United Kingdom. T (0)20 7700 6700 F (0)20 7700 8066 www.QuartoKnows.com

A catalogue record for this book is available from the British Library.

ISBN 978-1-78493-919-9

Based on the original story by Steve Smallman and Daniel Howarth
Author of adapted text: Katie Woolley
Series Editor: Joyce Bentley
Series Designer: Sarah Peden

Manufactured in Dongguan, China TL102017

9 8 7 6 5 4 3 2 1

MIX
Paper from responsible sources
FSC® C104723
www.fsc.org

**Reading
Gems**

# Go Away,
# Dot!

Max went out to play.

Dot can go out to play too.

Max saw Jack and Sam.

8

Dot went away.

Max, Jack and Sam played with the ball.

Dot went away to play.

The friends played high up
in the tree.

They kicked the ball up high.

15

The friends played
by the river.

This is fun.

Max, Jack and Sam looked
and looked for Dot.

Max saw Dot
in the tree.

22

Dot and Max played by the river.

# Story Words

ball

Dot

Jack

Max

play

river

Sam

tree

# Let's Talk About Go Away, Dot!

**Look carefully at the book cover.**

Who is in the picture?

Do you think the character looks happy or sad here?

How can you tell?

**Have a look at the dinosaurs in this picture.**

What game are the friends playing?

Does it look like fun?

What games do you like to play?

## Can you draw a dinosaur friend for Dot?

What would he or she look like?

## The story is about being kind.

Do you think Max and his friends were kind to Dot?

It's not nice to be left out. How do you think Dot feels?

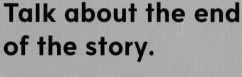

## Talk about the end of the story.

Did you like the ending?

What do you think the characters did next?

# Fun and Games

Look at the characters below.
Which one does not have the letter
'm' in their name?

Max

Mum

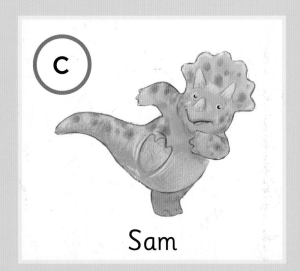

Sam

Dot

Answer: **d:** Dot.
**a:** Max, **b:** Mum and **c:** Sam all have the letter 'm'.

# Look at the items below.
## Can you find them in the picture?

# Your Turn

Now that you have read the story,
have a go at telling it in your own words.
Use the pictures below to help you.

# GET TO KNOW READING GEMS

**Reading Gems** is a series of books that has been written for children who are learning to read. The books have been created in consultation with a literacy specialist.

The books fit into four levels, with each level getting more challenging as a child's confidence and reading ability grows. The simple text and fun illustrations provide gradual, structured practice of reading. Most importantly, these books are good stories that are fun to read!

**Level 1** is for children who are taking their first steps into reading. Story themes and subjects are familiar to young children, and there is lots of repetition to build reading confidence.

**Level 2** is for children who have taken their first reading steps and are becoming readers. Story themes are still familiar but sentences are a bit longer, as children begin to tackle more challenging vocabulary.

**Level 3** is for children who are developing as readers. Stories and subjects are varied, and more descriptive words are introduced.

**Level 4** is for readers who are rapidly growing in reading confidence and independence. There is less repetition on the page, broader themes are explored and plot lines straddle multiple pages.

*Go Away, Dot!* follows a brother and sister as they learn to play nicely together. It explores themes of family, sibling arguments and kindness.

# Level 1

Max, Jack and Sam played with the ball.

Go away, Dot!

Dot went away to play.

Short sentences ✓

Simple vocabulary ✓

Lots of repetition ✓

Pictures and words support one another ✓